Changes,Changes

Changes, Changes

By PAT HUTCHINS

THE MACMILLAN COMPANY · NEW YORK

The art was prepared in four colors—black pen-and-ink line drawings and separate overlays for yellow, red and blue, with benday tones to make orange, green and gray.

For Elsie and Bob Bruce

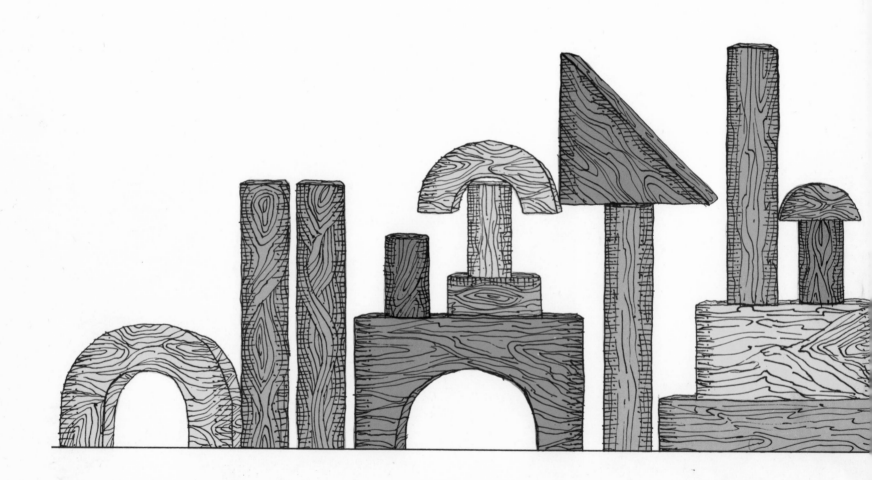

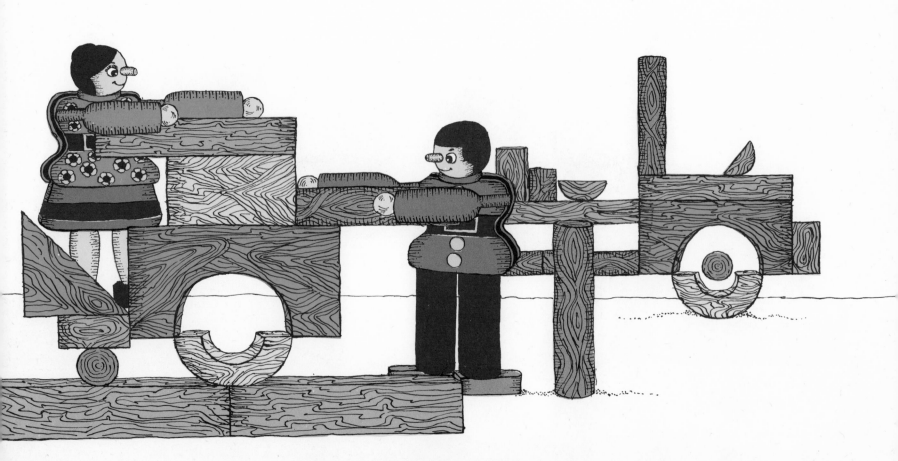

84566

DATE DUE

NO 19 '73	AP 21 '76	FEB. 11 '87
NO 23	MAY 15 '76	OCT 13 1987
11 '74	MAR 26	FACULTY
FE 11 '74	FEB 23	MAR. 06 1993
FE 27 '74	30 '80	MAR 20 1993
MR 22 '74	OCT 2 '81	
FE 18 '75	OCT 31 '81	OCT. 06 1994
D 2 '75	DEC 22 '81	SEP 21 2000
OC 7 '75	OCT 10 983	FEB 23 '04
OC 10 '75	OCT 20 1983	
NO 10 75	NOV 6 '84	
	OCT 20 '84 FEB 26 '04	23 0